This book belongs to:

T0117652

_____

penguins

1 2 3

penguins

123

KEVIN SCHAFER

NorthWord Press
Chanhassen, Minnesota

One little penguin
alone in the snow.

Somehow it always knows
which way to go.

1

Two penguins together
are better than one.

Having a friend
is always more fun!

2

3 Standing together
we add up to **three**.

If we add one more,
how many will we be?

Four penguins diving for their favorite dish.

Not soup, not spaghetti–
they really like fish!

To find their way home,
these **five** penguins know

exactly which way
they all have to go.

5

6

Six penguins
all in a row.

Do their feet
get cold
in the snow?

7

Six chicks and a grownup in very cold weather.

They add up to **seven**, all standing together.

When these **eight** penguins
want to go for a ride,

they simply get down
on their bellies and slide!

8

Have you ever wondered how penguins have fun?

These **ten** like standing out in the sun.

10

Not every penguin
lives on snow or on ice.

These **eleven** find
that the beach is quite nice.

11

Twelve penguins jumping–
that makes a dozen.

12

And each one
looks just like its cousin!

Can you count
how many penguins you see?

Are there twenty, or fifty,
or a hundred and three?

KEVIN SCHAFER is a wildlife photographer and writer who traveled to four continents and dozens of remote islands to gather the pictures for this book. He is also the author of *Penguin Planet*, recipient of the 2000 National Outdoor Book Award, and an enthusiastic grandfather. For more penguin information visit www.penguinplanet.com.